Dear Grandma

by Alma Flor Ada • illustrated by Sally Schaedler

≪Harcourt

Orlando   Boston   Dallas   Chicago   San Diego

Visit *The Learning Site!*

www.harcourtschool.com

November 2

Dear Grandma,

Thank you for the pencil case you sent! I put all my new pens and pencils inside it.

I miss you very much. I wish you were here so I could tell you face to face about school every day.

I would like to see the new colt. Are your chickens laying many eggs? Who will gather the eggs for you now that I'm not there?

I love you Grandma. I wish you could be here or I could be there.

Your grandson,

Tomás

November 11

Dear Grandma,

Thank you for your letter. School is not always fun here. There are so many things I don't understand.

The teacher wants us to make new friends. Yesterday she gave half of the class cards with one word on them. She gave the other half of the class cards with part of "The Star-Spangled Banner" written on them. We had to find the person who had the missing word. My card said:

"Oh, say can you see,
by the dawn's early   "

I have tried to sing "The Star-Spangled Banner,"
but I don't know all the words yet. I don't know what
they mean yet either. I didn't know what to do.
Finally, a girl who had a card with the word *light* on it
came over to me. Her name is Fabiola. She was born
in the United States, but her parents are from Spain.
She showed me her card, and we read the cards
together. I felt much better after that.

Then the teacher asked us to stand in a row and read each part of the song in order. I was nervous, but when Fabiola and I read our part together, we sounded strong. I hope I meet more nice friends like Fabiola.

Now we are learning about the American Revolution. Everyone but me seems to know who George Washington and Benjamin Franklin were. What should I do?

I miss you, Grandma. I would feel better if you were here.

Love,
Tomás

November 20

Dear Grandma,

Wow! Twenty new chicks — that's fantastic! I guess it was good that I wasn't there to gather the eggs. You decided to let them hatch instead.

When these chicks grow up, you will need a lot of help. There will be lots of eggs to gather from so many hens!

Thank you for suggesting that I find information about the American Revolution in the library.

The librarian, Mrs. Clark, smiled when I asked her my questions. She told me that George Washington was the first President of the United States. She said he was very brave and was a great leader and hero.

Mrs. Clark told me that Benjamin Franklin was known for his inventions. Did you know that he discovered electricity? He tied a key to a kite and flew it in a storm. Lightning struck the key, and Benjamin Franklin felt a jolt of electricity. Mrs. Clark said, "Don't try that at home!" I know what she means.

I checked out books about both leaders so I could learn more about them. Now I'll know what the teacher is talking about.

Thank you, Grandma. You help even when you are far away. I would rather have you here, though. I wish I could give you a big hug!

Your grandson,

Tomás

December 3

Dear Grandma,

Every time someone in our class yawns, my teacher says, "We may have a new Rip Van Winkle here."

I didn't know what she meant. The next time I went to the library, I asked Mrs. Clark, "What is a Rip Van Winkle?"

At first she couldn't understand me. I explained to her what my teacher had said. Then Mrs. Clark said, "Oh! You mean '*Who* is Rip Van Winkle?'"

She told me he was not a real person but a character in a story. He fell asleep for a very long time.

Now I understand why my teacher says, "We may have a new Rip Van Winkle here" when she sees a sleepy student.

I like learning new things. You and Mrs. Clark help me a lot.

Love,
Tomás

December 11

Dear Grandma,

Whenever I think I'm beginning to understand everything, I find new things I know nothing about.

Today my teacher talked about Johnny Appleseed. "We can all be like Johnny Appleseed," she said. "Let's plant good deeds like apple seeds as we go. We may not see the fruit that grows, but planting the good seed is the most important thing."

It sounds as if Johnny Appleseed did good things, but I don't know who he was. I felt bad because I was the only one who didn't know what the teacher was talking about.

Just then, Fabiola looked at me and smiled. Then she said to the teacher, "I think Tomás doesn't know who Johnny Appleseed was." The teacher looked surprised. Then she said, "Thank you, Fabiola. Maybe you can tell Tomás about Johnny Appleseed after school."

I'm glad Fabiola will explain this to me. Maybe I can ask her about other things, too.

Are you coming to visit soon? Let me know when you want me to help you take care of all those chickens!

Much love,
Tomás

December 13

Dear Grandma,

Remember Johnny Appleseed? Well, Fabiola and I
went to the library. After I talked to Fabiola and Mrs.
Clark, I learned all about Johnny Appleseed.

The next day, I went back to the library to thank
Mrs. Clark for her help. This time she told me about
some people in this country who had a hard time being
accepted.

She told me about Rosa Parks, an African American
woman who took an empty seat at the front of a bus.
The bus driver told her to sit at the back, where
African Americans were supposed to sit. Rosa Parks
refused. Then other people followed her example.

Then Mrs. Clark showed me a book about Jackie Robinson. He was the first African American to play on a major league baseball team. Most people didn't want African Americans to play major league sports. One day one of Jackie Robinson's white teammates, Pee Wee Reese, put his arm around Jackie right in the middle of the baseball field. That's when things began to change.

Now, when kids laugh at me because of my accent or because I forget English words, I can take it. I just think about people who have had a more difficult time than I have.

Love,
Tomás

December 19

Dear Grandma,
Today I finally learned all of the words to "The Star-Spangled Banner."

"Oh, say can you see by the dawn's early light

What so proudly we hail'd at the twilight's last gleaming?

Whose broad stripes and bright stars thro' the perilous fight

O'er the ramparts we watch'd were so gallantly streaming?

And the rockets' red glare, the bombs bursting in air,

Gave proof thro' the night that our flag was still there.

Oh, say does that star-spangled banner yet wave

O'er the land of the free and the home of the brave?"

When I see you again, I will sing it for you.

Love,
Tomás

December 29

Dear Grandma,

I put your sign, *Sí, se puede,* on my bedroom wall. I practice saying it in English — *Yes, I can!*

You asked me what I want to be when I grow up. I don't know yet, but I liked what my teacher said about Johnny Appleseed. I don't know what seeds I could plant. Maybe if I keep reading, I'll find out.

Dad is so happy to see me bringing books home from the library. He says I deserve a reward for working so hard in school.He promised that I could visit you as soon as school is over!

Your happy grandson,
Tomás